HALF
AND
HALF

KENNETH H. KIM

Artesian Press
P.O. Box 355 Buena Park, CA 90621

Take Ten Books
Sports

Other Take Ten Themes:
Mystery
Adventure
Disaster
Chillers
Thrillers
Fantasy

Project Editor:Liz Parker
Assistant Editor: Carol Newell
Cover Illustrator:Marjorie Taylor
Cover Designer: Tony Amaro
Text Illustrator:Fujiko Miller
©2000 Artesian Press

 _Artesian Press_

ISBN 1-58659-032-

Chapter 1

This story is supposed to be about basketball, but it's kind of about my family, too. Sometimes when you want to talk about one thing, you end up talking about everything.

Anyway, it all started with my first day in high school. The teacher was Mr. Ross, this bald-headed guy with glasses. He was walking around the room asking everyone to talk about their families and stuff. I was sitting way in the back with my head down, hoping and praying that he didn't call on me. Of course, he did, and then the whole class got really quiet because they all know I don't live with my parents. Mr. Ross smiled and said, "Go ahead, Nicky."

I didn't say anything. Maybe he'd get the picture and pick on someone else.

But he just said, "Why don't you start with your mother?"

He asked for it, I thought to myself. So I took a deep breath and began. "My mother was killed in a shipwreck off the coast of Africa," I told the class. "I was raised in the jungle by a tribe of savage apes." I heard giggles around the room and kept going. "My father was a Baptist preacher, a hard-working man of the land. He taught me right from wrong, good from evil. He ran off with another woman when I was seven."

Mr. Ross frowned and started to say something, but I kept going.

"My sister," I said, and the whole class laughed because they knew I didn't even have a sister, "was taken away on a spaceship by aliens from another galaxy when I was thirteen. She's worshipped as a goddess on their planet now."

Everyone was cracking up except for Mr. Ross. I was about to go on, but he grabbed me by the arm and dragged me out of the room and down to the counselor's office. Talk about a lousy sense of humor.

Since I'd just started high school, I hadn't met the counselor yet. At my old junior high, the counselor and I got to know each other pretty well. He used to always tell me I had a lot of potential, but that I had an "attitude problem." I don't think he was too crazy about me.

So I was surprised when this counselor turned out to be a lady. Her name was Ms. Kerner, and she was kind of cute even though she was pretty old, like in her thirties. Anyway, she was having a hard time reading my file, so I finally told her, "Look, you can't call my parents. I live with my two older brothers. You probably know Jamie." I was sure she knew Jamie. He was *always* in trouble.

"You're Jamie Shannon's brother?" she asked, surprise on her face.

"We don't look very much alike," I mumbled.

"Jamie's quite a character," she told me. That killed me. A character. Jamie's the craziest person I know, and he's my brother.

"So where are your parents?" Ms. Kerner asked.

"I don't know where my dad is. He and my mom have been divorced for as long as I can remember," I tried to explain. "My mom got remarried last year and moved away."

"Why didn't she take you with her?"

"Her new husband has a couple of kids from his previous marriage, and they live in this dinky little apartment. My brothers and I just decided to stay in our old house."

Ms. Kerner still couldn't figure it out. "How do you manage?" she asked.

"Mom sends us a check every month to help cover the bills. Sonny, my oldest brother, works and pays for everything else," I told her. "We get by."

"It must be difficult."

I shrugged. It kind of stunk, if you want to know the truth. But there was nothing I could do about it, so I didn't say anything.

Ms. Kerner looked at me and said, "Nicky, if you ever need someone to talk to, I want you to know you can come to me."

I just nodded. "Sure," was all I said.

Chapter 2

I went out into the hall while Ms. Kerner got on the telephone. A bunch of Chinatown kids were walking by, and I stared at my shoes until they passed.

They were pretty strange. They all wore the same kind of funky clothes, and most of the girls had fake curly hair—perms—and even some of the guys did, too. There's nothing dumber looking than a Chinese guy with curly hair.

They whispered and called me some name in Chinese that means half and half. It's like a swear word to them.

Ms. Kerner came out into the hall. "I called your brother, and he'll be here soon. I told him you were suspended for the rest of the day." She smiled at me like she just did me a big favor or something, so I smiled back and she left.

I was starting to get really depressed, sitting there by myself, when all of a sudden I heard Jamie's voice down the hall. He was with some of his friends. I figured they were cutting class, as usual. He stopped when he saw me.

"Dude," he said, squatting down in front of me, "what are you doing here?"

Jamie's a year ahead of me and two years younger than our older brother Sonny. He's really good-looking. He has the best possible combination of features from our Chinese and Irish heritage. He's tall and slim with big green eyes, a neat nose, and brown wavy hair. Sonny's bigger than Jamie but Sonny looks a little rougher: stiff black

hair, broader features, and thicker arms and legs. I look more Chinese than either of them, especially in the eyes. I'm tall and skinny.

"Bro," Jamie said again, tapping my knee, "what's going on?"

"I got suspended for the day," I told him. Jamie stared at me in disbelief. "One of my teachers didn't like what I said in class," I explained. "It's no big deal."

"Who was it? I'll—"

"It's okay, Jamie. It was my fault, anyway," I interrupted.

He nodded his head, still having a hard time believing that it was me, not him, who was in trouble. "I wouldn't want to be in your shoes," he grinned. "Sonny's going to kill you."

"I'll be all right."

"Okay." He started to walk away. "I don't want to catch you here again," he warned, turning back and shaking his finger at me. "You got that?"

I smiled. "You'd better get out of here," I told him. "I'll tell Sonny I saw you cutting class."

He laughed, and I watched him as he ran off and disappeared down the hallway with his friends.

"I don't know what's gotten into you," Sonny said as we were driving home.

"It was nothing, Sonny. I'm sorry they made you come all the way down here."

"What did you say to him?"

"I didn't say anything," I told Sonny. This wasn't really true, of course, but I felt pretty stupid about the whole thing already. Besides, I had the feeling Sonny wasn't going to find my little story any funnier than Mr. Ross did.

"You must have said something," Sonny said to me.

"Forget about it," I advised him.

"Can I go with you to the restaurant?" I asked quickly, before he could get mad at me.

Sonny's the manager at a restaurant by the airport. It's a great place. All the people there know I'm his little brother, so they give me free food and stuff.

"You're going home and studying for the rest of the day."

I sighed. Sonny wants me to go to college. I'm supposed to be the smart one in the family. "Come on, Sonny," I pleaded.

"Forget it, Nicky."

"I've got all of my books with me. I can study in the back of the restaurant."

He shook his head, but I could tell he was starting to give in.

"I don't want to be left in the house all by myself," I moped.

"Oh, all right," he said finally.

It was late and pitch black outside by the time we started to drive home.

I was rattling around in the front seat of Sonny's pick-up truck, trying not to fall asleep. I wondered what Jamie was doing, and then I thought about our mom.

"Do you think Mom's happier now, Sonny?" I asked.

"What do you mean?" He didn't look up from the road.

"Do you think she's glad that she has a real Chinese family now?" The guy she married is a Chinese banker with two perfect little Chinese kids.

"What are you talking about?"

"Well, *she's* Chinese, for Pete's sake," I said. It made perfect sense to me. I didn't know why Sonny couldn't understand.

"We'll always be her real kids."

"You think so?"

"Yeah. Nicky, you can't blame Mom and Dad for what we are. You just have to make the best of it."

The road was really bumpy, and I

was rocking back and forth in my seat. "It doesn't bug you?" I asked.

Sonny cleared his throat. "You just have to work hard, Nicky. If you work hard and become successful, people will accept you for what you are. That's the way the world is."

I was half asleep, and I kept banging my head against the window. "Do you think it bugs Jamie?"

Sonny laughed softly in the darkness. "I don't think anything bugs Jamie."

That's true, I thought to myself. Then I went to sleep before I could think of anything else.

Chapter 3

Sonny shook me awake when we got home, and I managed to find my way to my room and fall into bed. I was asleep for a little while, then I heard a car outside and Jamie's footsteps inside the house. I heard the refrigerator door open. I could imagine him getting a soda and making a sandwich.

It was true nothing bugged Jamie. He didn't think about being half Chinese or anything like that. The funny thing was, out of the three of us, he was the only one who knew anything of our Oriental culture: He was a black belt in *taekwondo*, some kind of Korean karate. And he was the one who acted like he wasn't Oriental at all! It was weird. But it gave him a tough reputation at school, because everyone knew he was a good fighter.

When I woke up in the morning and went out to the kitchen, Jamie was asleep on the couch.

Before Sonny goes to work he always wakes Jamie up and drags him out of bed so he'll get to school on time. But Jamie usually just falls asleep again after Sonny leaves.

I gave Jamie a shake as I walked by, and he began to open his eyes when he heard me in the kitchen.

"Do you want some eggs?" I asked.

"Sure." He yawned and sat down at the table. I made scrambled eggs, and he popped a couple of pieces of bread into the toaster.

"Do you ever think about Mom?" I asked him while we were eating breakfast. I didn't know why I was thinking about Mom so much. She'd been gone for more than a year.

"No," Jamie said.

"Why not?" I didn't know why I was surprised by his answer, but I was.

"Because she's not here," he answered simply. He got up and put his plate into the sink. He started to wash his hands and face.

"Jamie, don't use the kitchen sink to wash your face," I told him. "You know Sonny doesn't like that."

"What Sonny doesn't know won't hurt him." He grinned and socked me on the arm. A car horn honked outside. Jamie stopped punching me and went to get his jacket. I looked out the window. A pretty blonde girl was sitting in the car, waiting for him.

"See you later, dude," Jamie said to me as he headed out the door. "Stay out of trouble."

"You should talk," I called back, but he was already gone. I heard the screech of tires on gravel and the sound of their laughter as the car pulled away.

I walked to school slowly, wishing I didn't have to go. In high school it seemed like everyone had their own little clique, and I somehow missed out on the joining-up period. When Sonny was in school, he was on the football team, so he got along okay. Jamie looks and acts white, so he fits in fine. But I don't know where I belong.

I saw this movie on cable once, about a tribe of Indians who live in the jungle in South America. They called themselves "the invisible people" because they thought the paint on their bodies made them invisible.

Sometimes I feel like I must be one of the invisible people. I can walk around school all day, and it seems like no one sees me or notices me. Today I'm so busy pretending I'm invisible that I don't notice at first that someone's trying to talk to me. Brendan, a short Chinatown guy who's in my gym class, has squeezed next to me in the crowded hallway.

"What is it?" I asked, startled.

"Can I talk to you for a second, Nicky?"

"Sure." I stepped out of the flow of traffic. "What's up?" I glanced around to see if anyone was looking at us. Will they think I'm a Chinatown dude because they see me talking to one of them? I ran my tongue over my lips.

"We're having a basketball tournament in Chinatown and we were wondering if you'd play on the team," Brendan said to me.

"Me?" I asked.

Brendan nodded. "You're pretty good. I've played with you in gym before. And you're tall," he added. "Especially for a Chinese."

"You know," I said slowly, "I'm only half—"

"That's okay," Brendan said quickly. "You *look* Chinese."

"Well, that's true," I had to agree. Brendan laughed.

"Okay?" he asked.

"Okay," I said.

Chapter 4

After school, I called Sonny to tell him I'd be home late, then I met Brendan at the bus stop. He introduced me to the other Chinatown guys. They all nodded and smiled, but they were too cool to talk to me. As I was standing on the curb with Brendan, Lori Demarest cruised by in her jeep with a bunch of her girlfriends.

"She is so fine," I told Brendan. He shrugged.

"She's all right for a —," he said, saying the word that means "white person" in Chinese. Actually, it means "ghost" or "spirit" and they use it almost as an insult, like the word they call me and my brothers.

I felt strange for a minute, thinking about that. Then the bus came and Brendan and I found a seat in the back.

The Chinatown in our city is really small, only a few square blocks, and it seems to be made up mostly of restaurants, little shops, and old apartments. Sonny used to bring Jamie and me down here to eat once in awhile. That was a long time ago, before Sonny started working, and before Jamie turned wild.

At the corner where the big downtown shopping mall ends and Chinatown starts, all of the Chinatown kids got off the bus, and I followed along.

The gym was in a big, old, rickety building. Inside, though, the wood floors shone and the rims were straight and tight. A group of younger boys had been practicing before us. They cleared the floor when we arrived, leaving the bright orange basketballs rolling on the court.

There were enough guys for two full teams. We ran through an organized practice. I was the only one who didn't know all of the drills and plays, and I felt slow and clumsy at first. But I was the tallest player in the gym, and that always counts for something when you're playing basketball. By the end of the two hours, I was catching on and fitting in pretty well with the second team.

"You play pretty well, Nicky," Howie said in the locker room after we finished playing. He was the best player on the team—a skinny, long-legged forward with a smattering of freckles around his nose. I didn't even know Chinese people had freckles.

"We need someone tall like you," he told me. "I like the way you block shots," he grinned. "Get that out of here!" he said, swatting at an imaginary ball. He laughed and tugged at the laces of his high-tops. "We'll have to get you a t-shirt."

All the other guys were wearing green "Chinatown Basketball" t-shirts. Brendan nudged me with his elbow and smiled.

After we showered and changed, Howie suggested that we wait for the girls. But everyone was too hungry, so we decided to eat first. We filed into a small restaurant with booths on each side and an aisle down the middle, like the car of a train.

The mother of one of the guys on the team ran the restaurant. She came out and said hello to everyone. She set up a big, round table near the back for us, and we all managed to scrunch in together. Some of the waitresses came over to our table, and the guys flirted with them.

Howie ordered in Chinese, and everyone else started talking in Chinese.

I was lost, since I can't understand more than a couple of words here and there.

Our first dish arrived at the table, a big bowl of steaming soup. It looked like hot and sour soup to me, but I wasn't sure. I was afraid to ask and look even more stupid and out of place than I already was. But I was happy for an excuse not to talk, so I swallowed down a big spoonful of the soup. It felt like I'd poured thousands of tiny pieces of glass down my throat. This soup was hotter than anything I'd ever tasted before. I needed to cough so badly that tears started to come out of my eyes, but I wouldn't let myself.

I looked around for a glass of water, but there was no water anywhere on the table. I took a gulp from the little cup of green tea sitting in front of me. But it was hot, too, and it only made my throat worse. I couldn't fight back the cough any longer. Brendan looked over at me.

"Are you all right, man?" he asked. All of the guys turned to look at me. I opened my mouth to say that I was fine, but only a croak came out. Everyone laughed, and I sank down in my chair. Howie patted me on the back.

"We'll make a Chinese out of you yet," he said happily.

Sonny was already asleep by the time I got home. I brushed my teeth as quietly as I could and went to bed. I fell asleep right away for the first time since Mom went away. I didn't wake up once during the night, not even when Jamie came in.

For the next week, I caught the bus downtown with the rest of the Chinatown kids and practiced with them every day after school. I felt myself getting more comfortable on the court after each afternoon. By Thursday I was practicing with the first team. Saturday was the day of the tournament, so on Friday we had drills and a short scrimmage and then a meeting in the locker room. Howie read off the starting five. I was the center. Brendan congratulated me and handed me a green "Chinatown Basketball" t-shirt and matching pair of shorts.

"Now we can tell you're on our team," he laughed. Howie passed out packages to everyone. I opened mine. Inside was a warm-up suit, green with white stripes down the sides and zippers at the bottom of the pants.

"Wow," I said softly. "Who pays for these?"

Brendan tried his on. "Some of the local businesses sponsor us," he told me. "They do it for the girls' teams and the junior teams, too."

I turned the jacket around. Written on the back was "Chinatown Express" in white block letters.

"That's us," said Howie, coming over. "We're the Express."

"Yeah! The Express!" Brendan shouted. He and Howie traded high fives. I laughed as I watched them.

Brendan said, "Come on, man!" and we all jumped up together and touched hands.

Chapter 5

After I got off the bus, I ran all the way home. I could hardly wait to show Sonny and Jamie my new stuff. They were watching TV when I came hurrying in through the front door. Sonny blinked sleepily and sat up on the couch.

"What have you been up to, Nicky?" he asked. "We haven't seen you all week."

I sat down on the couch between him and Jamie. "I'm playing basketball for the Chinatown team in their tournament," I told him.

"Chinatown?" they both said at the same time.

"Yeah, look at all this stuff I got." I

opened up my duffel bag and took out the uniform and warm-ups. "Isn't it cool?"

"Chinatown Express?" said Sonny, holding up the jacket. "How did you get mixed up in this?"

"They asked me to play for them," I said, looking at him and then Jamie. "Because I'm tall—for a Chinese person."

"Are you sure you know what you're doing, little bro?" Sonny asked.

"It's fun," I told him. "They're all really nice. Don't you think this is great?" I said to Jamie. "They gave me all this stuff, and I get to wear it at the tournament."

Jamie scratched his head. "Chinatown?" he said again.

"I'm glad you're having fun," yawned Sonny as he got up from the couch. "Just don't get into any trouble down there."

"The tournament's tomorrow," I

said quickly, because he was getting ready to go to sleep. "Do you guys want to come down and watch me play?"

"I have to work tomorrow," Sonny apologized. "Sorry." He walked into the kitchen. I looked at Jamie.

"Are you kidding?" he said. "I'm not going to hang out with all those freaks."

"They're not freaks, Jamie," I told him. "They're nice. They're nicer than the people you hang out with."

Jamie shook his head. "I wouldn't be caught dead with those Chinatown geeks."

"They're more like us than you think."

"If you lie down with dogs, you wake up with fleas," he said to me, like he was a teacher or something.

"You just think being white is better than anything else," I said angrily. "You buy into all that trash you see on

TV and read in magazines. Mom used to tell us it was all bull, and she was right."

"Mom didn't know what she was talking about," Jamie said, getting madder by the second. "I'm not buying into anything. It's the way things are, plain and simple. And if you want to move up in the world, you'd better open your eyes, kid."

"Shut up! Both of you!" We turned to look at Sonny standing in the doorway of the kitchen. I'd never seen him look so angry. He was almost shaking. "I don't want to hear that kind of talk from either of you!" he shouted at us. "If you have a problem with what we are, it's in your head. Deal with it. You got that?"

"I don't have to deal with anything," Jamie shot back. He grabbed his jacket off the back of the chair and walked out of the house, slamming the door behind him. I looked at Sonny.

"I'm sorry, Sonny."

He came over and ruffled my hair with his hand.

"It's not your fault, Nicky. I'm sorry I yelled at you. Just ... go out and have a good time tomorrow, okay?"

I nodded and blinked back my tears. He smiled and patted me on the head again.

"Goodnight, Nicky."

I watched him as he walked down the hall to his bedroom. "Goodnight, Sonny," I whispered.

Chapter 6

I took the bus down to Chinatown early the next morning and met the other guys in the locker room. The gym was filled with Chinese boys and girls, all in different colored warm-up suits, shooting baskets and running up and down the court. I'd never seen so many Chinese people in one place before. Brendan told me the different teams come from Chinatowns everywhere.

I saw warm-up jackets for teams from all over the country. Some of the teams wore their hair long. Some had their hair short in front and long in the back. Still others had theirs styled to look like there was a little tail in back, and they clipped colorful feathers to the end of the tail.

My team took the floor to warm up, and I felt weak and nervous. The girls from our Chinatown sat behind our bench and cheered for us. We went over to the sideline one more time before the game started. As I ran onto the court, one of the girls yelled good luck to me in Chinese.

We won the first game. I did okay, even though it was my first basketball game with referees and uniforms and people watching and everything. The other team played really rough, but they were short, even shorter than the guys on my team. I played well, blocking shots, grabbing rebounds, and even scoring a few easy baskets.

We made it all the way to the semifinals and had to face a team from Boston, the Dragons.

"Best Chinatown team in the country," Brendan whispered to me while we were getting ready. I watched them run onto the floor. They were city kids, wiry, tall, all of them talking trash.

"Hey you big geek," one of them yelled at me, his long hair tied back in a ponytail, "I'm coming right at you. In your *face.*"

They were faster, more athletic, and they built up a big lead at halftime. Our team was exhausted, our t-shirts wet and heavy with sweat.

Little by little, we came back. Howie made an impossible shot as he was being fouled. He hit the foul shot afterwards, and we took the lead. They had time for one more play. The ponytail kid came off a screen, caught the pass, and drove the lane. He leaped high and switched hands in midair, trying to lay the ball in off the glass. I went up with him, and we hung in the air for what seemed like forever, like in a dream.

Finally I swatted at the ball, and it played off the backboard, bouncing away harmlessly. The buzzer sounded to end the game. We'd won!

After the game, I sat in the stands with Brendan to watch the other games and wait for our next one. Howie came over, a frown on his freckled face.

"I have some bad news, Nicky," he told me.

"What is it?"

"One of the other teams is filing a protest because you're not all Chinese. They say we'll have to forfeit our games if we let you play."

"Can they do that?" asked Brendan. Howie looked at him and nodded.

"That's what the rules say."

"Can't we do anything about it?" Brendan asked him.

"Forget it," I told them. "I don't want you guys to get into any trouble because of me."

"There really isn't anything we can do," Howie said. I nodded and didn't say anything. "I'm sorry, Nicky," he said. He patted me on the knee, got up, and walked away. I watched him as he went down the steps. He had a slightly bow-legged, athletic walk. Brendan shook his head.

"That stinks, man. You know what it was? You were just too good."

I tried to smile. "It's okay," I told him.

"Why don't you stick around?" he said. "There's going to be a dance afterwards."

I told him I'd think about it, but I knew I wouldn't. The tournament was over for me.

Chapter 7

The ball bounced high off the rim. I timed my jump perfectly and tapped the ball into the basket while I was still up in the air. As we ran back the other way, I sneaked a peek over at the sidelines to see if the coach saw my play. But he was too busy talking to some older players to notice. I swore silently under my breath. I wasn't even sure what I was doing there anymore. I must have lost my mind.

What happened was that I got this crazy idea that I really missed playing basketball. Then I got the even crazier idea to ask the school basketball coach if I could try out for the team. So there I was, practicing with some of the sec-

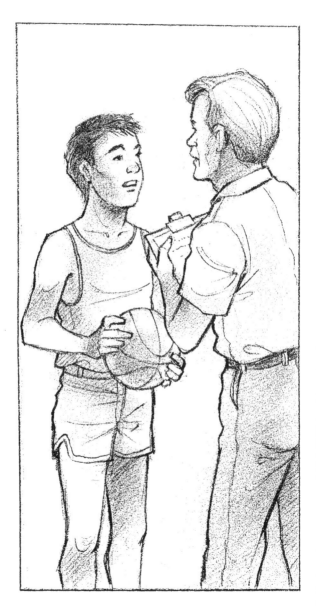

ond-stringers. The weirdest part of the whole thing was that I was actually playing pretty well. I could see the surprise on the faces of the players, like, "Who is this guy?"

All I knew was that for the first time in my life, I'd found something where I could make a difference. If I tried my hardest, I could make things happen.

The ball rolled loose on the floor, and I dove for it. I batted it over to one of my teammates, who took off in the other direction on a fast break.

Coach Burton frowned and scratched his chin as he studied his clipboard. Practice was over, and everyone else had gone into the locker room except for me. He called me over for a little talk. I wiped my face with my t-shirt and waited for him to say something.

He was a short guy, with a thin face and small, yellow teeth like a rat's. He must have been a guard when he was in high school.

"Who did you say you played for again?" he asked at last.

"The Chinatown team," I said.

"What position?"

"Center."

He frowned again. "Well," he said, "you're not going to be able to play center for this team. You're just not tall enough."

I had told myself not to get my hopes up. I had told myself that over and over, but my heart still sank at his words.

"Thanks for giving me a shot," I said, turning away.

"Are you interested in trying a new position? The Junior Varsity team could use a big guard," he grinned. "You think you can learn how to handle the ball?"

"Definitely!"

"You have a lot of catching up to

do," he warned. "It's not going to be easy."

"Nothing's *ever* easy for me," I said with a smile. "I'm used to it."

He laughed and slapped me on the back. "I like your attitude, kid," he said. "I like your attitude."

Chapter 8

I took the porch steps two at a time and threw open the screen door. I tossed my books on the couch as I headed for the kitchen.

"Hey, Sonny," I shouted happily. I smelled dinner cooking inside. "Guess what—," I stopped dead in my tracks. Sonny came out of the kitchen. His face was as white as a sheet. Mom was with him. I stood there, staring, like I couldn't believe what I was seeing.

"Mom?" I said, so softly that I could barely hear myself.

She smiled at me. "You're so tall now, Nicky."

I wanted to run up to her and hug her so badly. I wanted to tell her how much I'd missed her, to tell her about the Chinatown guys, about basketball, about everything. But I didn't. I just stood there for some reason, as still as a stone.

"What are you doing here?" was all I could say.

"I wanted to tell you the good news in person," she said. "We bought a house, a big house, over across the river. We have enough room for the whole family now."

"You want us to live with you?"

"Of course," she said. "I want all of my boys back home with me." She looked over at Sonny. "Even if some of them think they're too big for that."

Sonny walked back into the kitchen. Mom turned to me again.

"Don't I even get a hug from my baby?" she asked. I went to her and leaned over to give her a hug. My throat was so tight I couldn't even say a single word.

I heard the screen door open behind me and Sonny's footsteps on the porch. It was cold, so I zipped my sweatshirt all the way up. He sat down beside me on the top stair. We were quiet for a long time, just looking up at the black sky.

"How come you don't want to go live with Mom?" I finally asked.

"I'm an old guy, Nicky," he sighed. "I mean, I'm out of school. I have a job, a car. I don't need to live at home any-more." He mussed my hair. "I'm a grown-up."

"Do you think Jamie's going to come back?"

Sonny shook his head and looked out into the darkness. "I don't know. He took off as soon as Mom got here. He didn't even want to talk to her."

"I guess things bug Jamie more than we thought."

"I guess so," Sonny said softly.

"What are you doing out here?"

I opened my eyes and looked up sleepily. Jamie was standing over me, pushing the toe of his boot into my side. I sat up and rubbed my eyes.

"I was waiting for you," I said.

"Out on the porch?" he asked, sitting down. "You're probably frozen solid."

"Yeah," I shivered. "It's cold."

"I thought you were supposed to be smart," he said.

"Not always," I admitted. "Where did you go?"

"Nowhere. I just didn't want to be around when Mom was here."

"Why not?" I asked.

"I don't know," he shrugged. "I just didn't."

"She wants us to come live with her, you know," I said to Jamie.

"I know. Did Sonny tell you that you could go with her if you want to?"

"Yeah, he did. Is that what he told

you?"

Jamie nodded. "Sonny's cool."

"But you're not going to go, are you?" I asked.

"No," said Jamie. "I'm not."

"Why not?" I asked.

Jamie stared at the wall. "I know you want things to be the way they used to, Nicky. But they can't be." He looked at me. "Things can't ever be the same."

For no reason at all, I started crying. Jamie shook me gently, trying to get me to stop. I fought back the tears.

"I made the J.V. basketball team, you know," I sniffled.

"All right, dude. I always knew you were okay. You've just got to stop worrying about trying to fit in. No one fits in, man. No one."

I was still crying, not big sobs or anything, but I could feel the tears running down my face. I just couldn't stop myself. "Can I stay here with you and

Sonny?" I asked.

"Sure," said Jamie. "But why would you want to?"

"We're brothers," I said. "We have to stick together."

Jamie laughed and wrapped his arm around my neck. "You're going to have to tell Mom, you know."

"I know." I wiped my eyes with the back of my hand. "She'll understand. I'll tell her I don't want to lose my spot on the school basketball team."

Jamie nodded. We were both quiet for awhile, just sitting there. Then we heard footsteps out in the darkness, and we squinted to see who was coming up to the house.

"Yo, Nicky," said Brendan. He was carrying a duffel bag in one hand, and Howie was at his side.

Jamie jumped to his feet. "Get out of here, before I cause you both some pain. You've caused enough trouble."

"Jamie, it's all right," I told him,

pushing him back. "I can handle this."

"Are you sure?" he asked.

"Yeah. I'll just be a few minutes."

Jamie shot Brendan and Howie one last dirty look before he went inside.

"What's up?" I asked them.

Brendan reached into his bag. "We brought you something," he said.

He pulled out a gleaming trophy and handed it to me. I stared. It was for first place at the Chinatown tournament.

"We won, man," Howie said. "We couldn't have done it without you."

"But I thought—" I started to stutter.

"We're going to talk to the league about changing the rules," Howie went on. "What they did to you wasn't fair."

I didn't know what to say, so I didn't say anything.

"I heard you made the J.V. team," Brendan said. "That's so cool."

"I learned a lot working out with

you guys," I admitted.

Howie shrugged. "You just needed a chance to play."

They started down the stairs. Then Brendan stopped and turned around. "We need you for the next tournament, man. Are you going to be around?"

I smiled. "Yeah," I told them. "I'm going to be around."